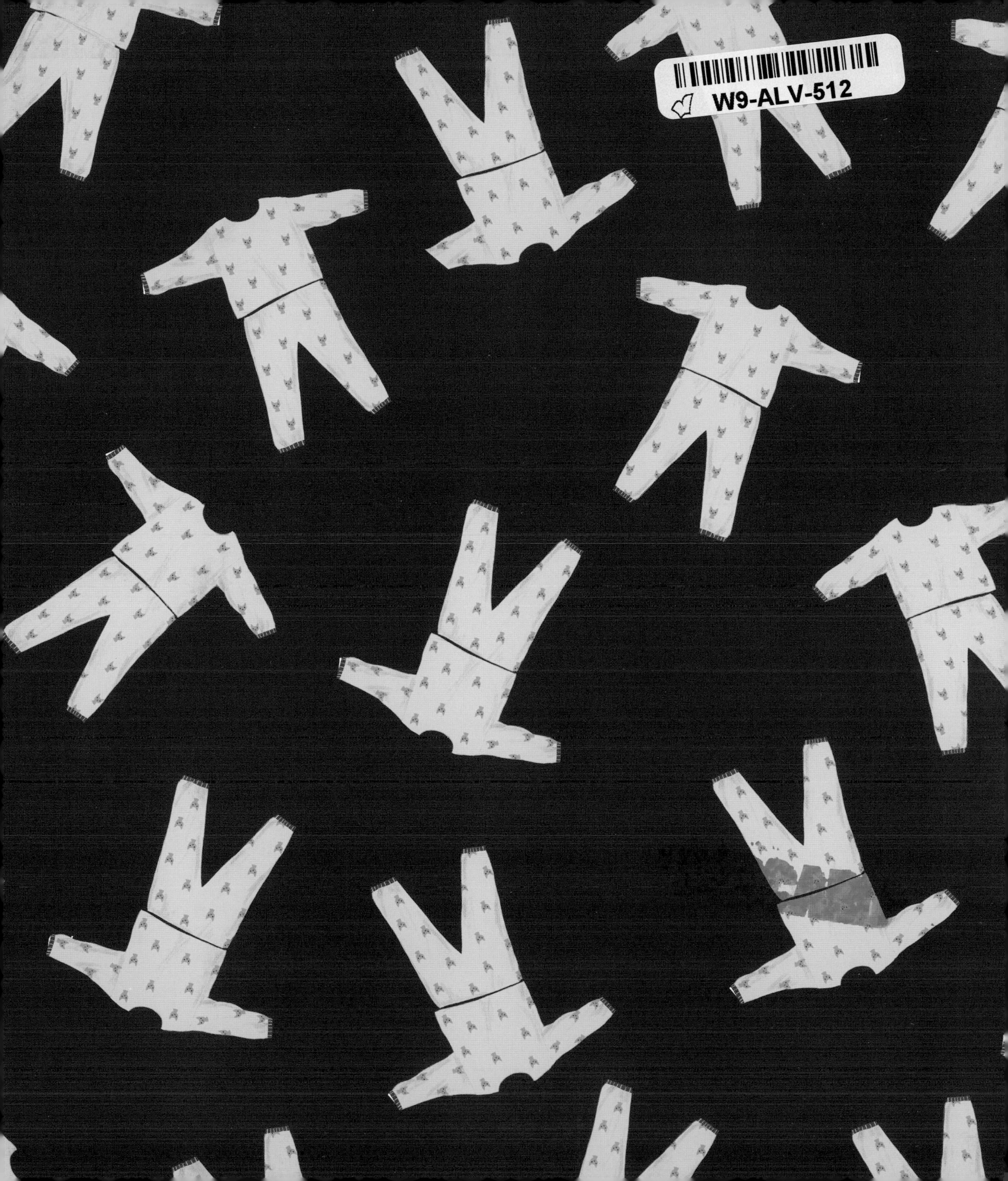

For Honor—A. McQ.

For Lianna and Nathanael, with love—R. B.

2021 First US Edition
Text copyright © 2021 by Anna McQuinn
Illustrations copyright © 2021 by Rosalind Beardshaw

Published by Charlesbridge
9 Galen Street
Watertown, MA 02472
(617) 926-0329
www.charlesbridge.com

First published in the United Kingdom and Ireland by Alanna Max,
38 Oakfield Road, London N4 4NL, United Kingdom, as *Lulu's Sleepover*.
Copyright © 2021 by Anna McQuinn
www.annamcquinn.com

Library of Congress Cataloging-in-Publication Data
Names: McQuinn, Anna, author. | Beardshaw, Rosalind, illustrator.
Title: Lola sleeps over / Anna McQuinn; illustrated by Rosalind Beardshaw.
Description: First US edition. | Watertown, MA: Charlesbridge Publishing,
    2021. | Series: Lola reads | Audience: Ages 2-5. | Audience: Grades K-1. |
    Summary: "Lola is excited for her first-ever sleepover at her cousin
    Hani's house where together they play, learn, and try new things."
    —Provided by publisher.
Identifiers: LCCN 2020026143 (print) | LCCN 2020026144 (ebook) |
    ISBN 9781623542917 (hardcover) | ISBN 9781632899248 (ebook)
Subjects: CYAC: Sleepovers—Fiction. | African Americans—Fiction.
Classification: LCC PZ7.M47883 Lt 2021 (print) | LCC PZ7.M47883 (ebook) |
    DDC [E]—dc23
LC record available at https://lccn.loc.gov/2020026143
LC ebook record available at https://lccn.loc.gov/2020026144

Printed in China
(hc) 10 9 8 7 6 5 4 3 2 1

Display type set in KG Life Is Messy by Kimberly Geswein and
    Graphen by Maciej Wloczewski
Text type set in Billy by David Buck at SparkyType
Color separations by Colourscan Print Co Pte Ltd, Singapore
Printed by 1010 Printing International Limited in Huizhou,
    Guangdong, China
Production supervision by Jennifer Most Delaney
Designed by Jon Simeon

Lola Sleeps Over

Anna McQuinn

Illustrated by Rosalind Beardshaw

ini Charlesbridge

Tonight is Lola's first sleepover!
Lola has visited
her cousin Hani lots of times,
but she has never stayed overnight.

Lola wants to wear
her favorite kanga dress.
She chooses what else to bring.

Lola packs her leggings for jumping.
She packs her overalls for building.
Lola and Hani will be dancing, too.

Her twirly dress and sparkly shoes
are essential for that.

Lola packs her cat pajamas
and her best books.
Mary and Dinah go on top.
Lola is ready.

Hani's house is just around the corner.
Lola and her daddy walk there.

Auntie Zari welcomes them.

Hani and Auntie Jina
are making lemonade.
Lola can't wait to taste it.

Daddy kisses everyone goodbye.
He will be back in the morning.

Hani and Lola play in Hani's rain forest.

They build bridges
and make a waterfall.
It is awesome.

Then Hani and Lola make water pictures.
They paint the whole wall . . .

and each other!

Hani and Lola play dress-up
after lunch. Now Lola is Hani . . .

and Hani is Lola!

Auntie Jina has made
Hani's favorite salad for dinner.

Lola has never liked cucumbers,
but these ones are delicious!

There is just enough time
for a movie before bed.

Hani's bed is magical.
Lola takes out Mary and Dinah.

Auntie Zari has a surprise.
It is a photo album
of when Auntie Zari
and Lola's daddy were little.

Auntie Zari tells them
a special bedtime story
about the photos.

Good morning!
It is time for Hani and Lola
to wake up.

Hani loves French toast.
Auntie Jina makes some as a treat.
Lola tries it. *Mmmm*! Delicious!

Ding-dong! It is Daddy already.
He has come to pick up Lola.

Lola loved her sleepover.
Soon it will be Hani's turn
to come to Lola's house.
Lola can't wait!